MARC BROWN

The Good Sport

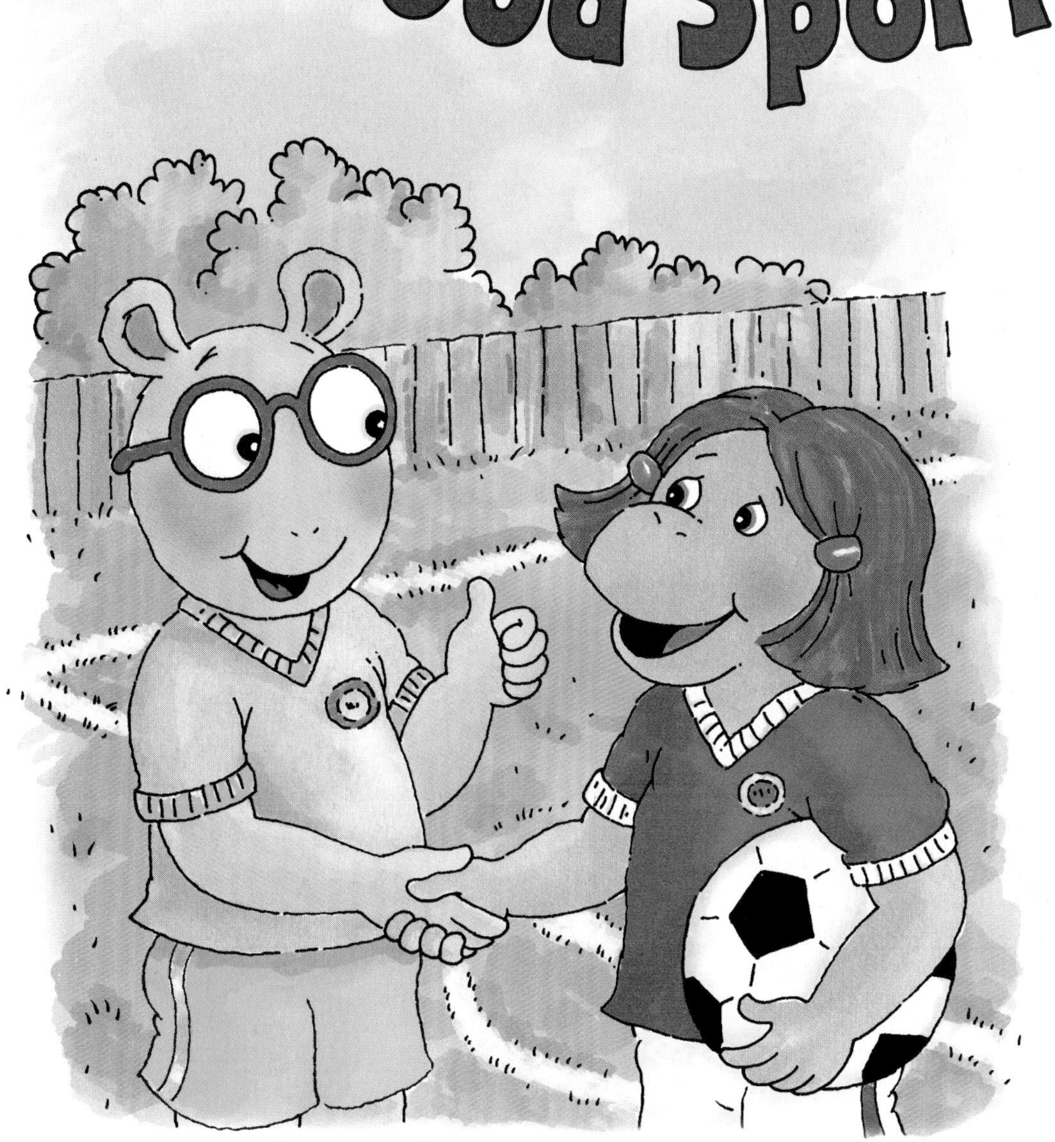

"Today's a big day!" said Dad.

It was the first Saturday of the soccer season. Arthur's dad was the new coach.

"Big deal," said Arthur. "Francine's team always beats us."

"It's not important if you win or lose," said Dad. "Just have fun!"

The kids picked team captains.

"I'll be captain of the red team," said Francine.

"We've elected Arthur as our captain," said the Brain.

"I've never been a captain before," said Arthur.

"You'll make a great captain," said Dad.

But Arthur wasn't so sure.

"Time to choose team names," said Francine.

"How about the Hot Dogs?" said Buster.

"Nope," Francine said.

"What about the Rubies?" offered Prunella.

"Nope," said Francine. "We'll be the Robins."

"*We* could be the Bulldogs," suggested Binky.

"Our uniforms are gray," said the Brain. "Bulldogs aren't gray."

The only gray animal Arthur could think of was Mr. Ratburn's pet hamster, Herman.

"How about the Hamsters?" said Arthur.

"Cool," said Binky.

During the first practice game, everybody was making goals.

The score was tied, until Francine kicked a ball into the net and it bounced off Binky's head.

"Foul!" yelled Arthur.

"No way!" shouted Francine. "We scored! We win!"

"I knew we would lose," said Arthur on the way home.

"That was just practice," said Dad. "The real game is next week."

The next Saturday, Arthur bounced out of bed. This time, his team was going to beat the Robins—no matter what.

But on the field, it was a different story. Francine raced in and out of Arthur's defense, scoring two more goals.

"Look!" shouted Arthur. "The Bionic Bunny is in the bleachers!"

"Where?" said Buster, spinning around to get a good look.

Arthur kicked the ball and scored.

"We win!" shouted the Brain. "Way to go!"

"You tricked him!" cried Francine. "That doesn't count."

"Face it," said Arthur. "We won!"

"You just wait until the next game," said Francine.
Then she gave a cheer:

"We are the Robins, so watch us soar.
Arthur's Hamsters will never score.
We'll ace this season—we always do.
Why you ask? 'Cause we're better than you!"

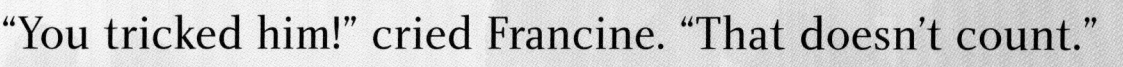

Then Fern did a cheer for her team:

"Hooray for the Hamsters, small and furry,
We can run and we can scurry.
Francine's Robins are no threat.
We'll win this season—that's no sweat!"

"You're history," shouted Francine.

"You wish," said Arthur.

"Now, Arthur, be a good sport," said Dad.

"It's just a game," said Coach Frensky.

By the next week, the whole town filled the bleachers, cheering and waving banners.

"You Robins better hide from our Hamsters!" shouted Grandma Thora.

"No way! The Robins rule!" called Mrs. McGrady.

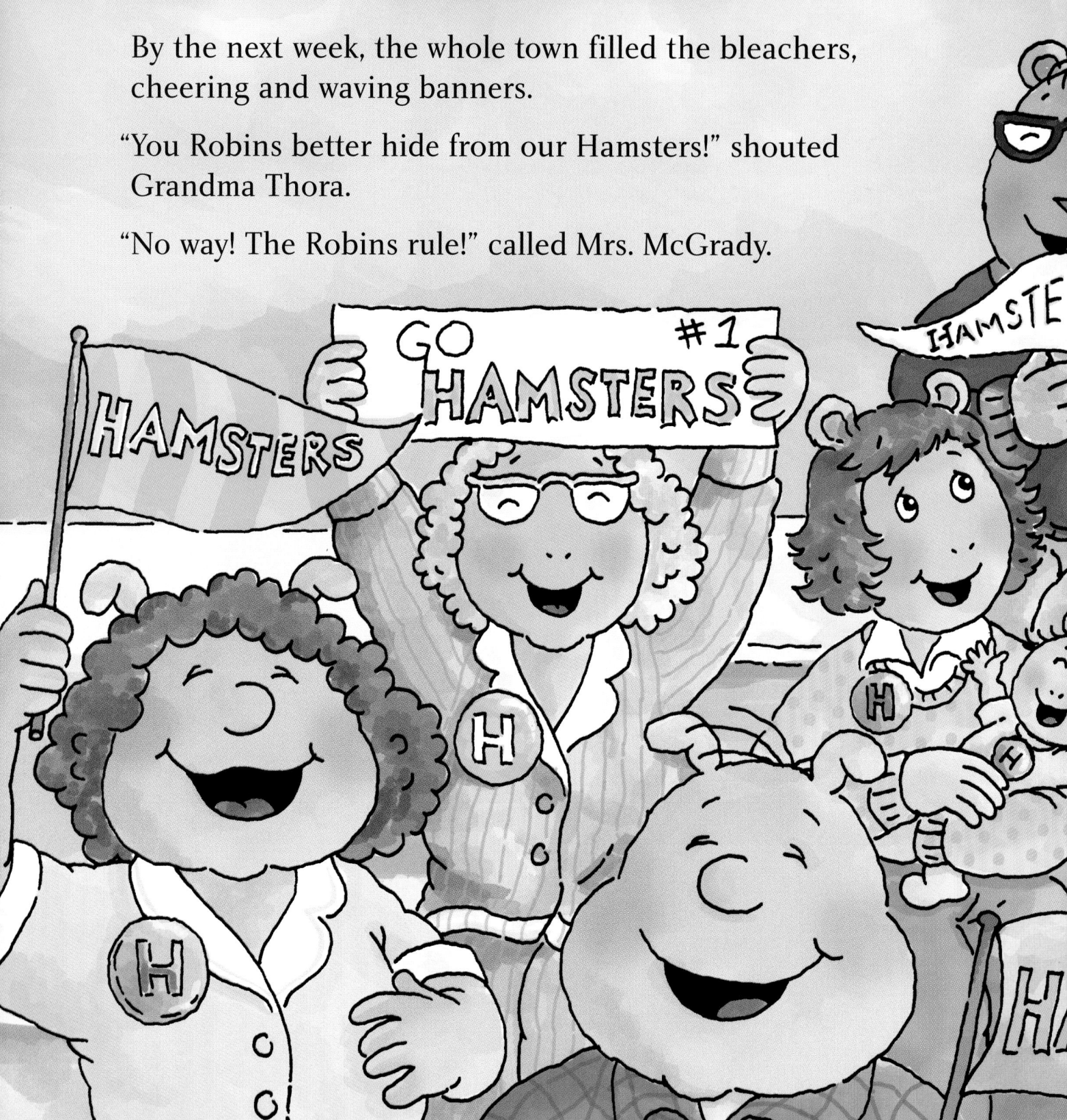

Everyone was shouting for their favorite team.

The game was tied, and the two coaches huddled with their teams.

"We can win," said Arthur's dad. "Let's get those Robins!"

"I thought you said winning didn't matter," said Arthur.

But Arthur's dad wasn't listening. "Come on, team!" he cried. "Let's give it the old one-two, heave-ho, get-up, and go-go-go!"

Francine had the ball. The only thing between her and the winning goal...was Arthur. Francine stared at Arthur. Arthur glared back.

The crowd and the coaches went wild.

"What are you waiting for?" Coach Frensky yelled. "Score! Score!"

"You tell 'em, Coach!" cried Buster's mom, biting her nails nervously.

"Kick the ball, Francine!" yelled Mrs. Frensky.

"Defense! Defense!" shouted Arthur's dad.

Francine and Arthur stopped and looked at the coaches.

Coach Frensky called a time out. "What's the matter with you two?" he asked.

Arthur's dad ran over to the bench.

"You grown-ups look so silly," said Arthur.

"You're taking this game much too seriously," laughed Francine.

"It is just a game," said Arthur.

"I guess we did get a *little* carried away," admitted Coach Frensky.

The game started up again. Francine scored the winning goal.

"You did it again!" said Arthur. "You're amazing!"

"Good game!" said Francine.

The coaches shook hands.

"Both teams are invited back to our house for a cookout celebration," announced Arthur's dad.

Everyone cheered.

At the cookout, Arthur piled everything on his hamburger. "This is the best burger ever!" he said.

Francine piled hers higher. "Mine is better!" she said.

"Is not!" cried Arthur.

Everyone laughed. But Francine and Arthur laughed the loudest of all.